Music is
NOT
banned!

GirlFriendZ
Pirate DJ
by Roger Hurn
Illustrated by Kenny Kiernan

Published by Ransom Publishing Ltd.
Radley House, 8 St. Cross Road, Winchester, Hampshire
SO23 9HX, UK
www.ransom.co.uk

ISBN   978 178127 152 0
First published in 2013

GirlFriendZ

Pirate DJ

Roger Hurn

Illustrated by Kenny Kiernan

Ransom

Kelly Montez

Like · Comment · Friend

Hey, I'm Kelly Montez, and unless you've been living in a cave for the past year you'll know I'm in the band *GirlFriendZ*.

Yeah, that's right, I'm the one with the killer looks and a voice like gravel dipped in honey. And *GirlFriendZ* is the number one band in the world – or it *was*, until the day the aliens invaded Earth and banned music! Those creepoids are *so* not cool.

But don't worry guys, we're not going to let them get away with that. *GirlFriendZ* will carry on making music and there's no way a bunch of alien weirdos in MIB (Music is Banned) is going to stop us!

Yaz Jackson

Like · Comment · Friend

Hiya guys, Yaz here. I was born in a circus and my mum and dad were acrobats, so that's why I'm always doing somersaults, cartwheels and back flips on stage. On our next tour I'm gonna walk across the stage on a high wire! How cool is that?

Yeah, you did hear me right. There WILL be another *GirlFriendZ* tour – just as soon as we find a way to send the Zargons back to their home planet with their creepy alien tails between their legs.

Olivia Parsons

Like · Comment · Friend

Hi *GirlFriendZ* fans. My name is Olivia – but everyone calls me Liv. I know I look like the girl next door, but I can be a bit of a wild child when it comes to music! I just love getting up on stage and singing my heart out!

But now those freaky aliens are arresting musicians and destroying all the musical instruments they can get their tentacles on! It makes me so mad, but they'll never catch us and stop us singing.

That's a promise!

Eve Rossi

Like · Comment · Friend

Hello everybody. I'm Eve, the girl with the crazy hair and the personality to match!

It's great being in *GirlFriendZ* 'cos it gives me the chance to wear all kinds of amazing outfits. I love designing my own clothes and it gives me a buzz when I see you guys copying my look!

I know the Zargons are trying to stop us having fun – but don't fret guys, we are *so* gonna have the last laugh!

Charlotte Opirah

Like · Comment · Friend

OK, it's me, Charlotte. Usually I'd rather sing than talk, 'cos I'm the best singer in the band. Hey, just kidding!!

But I've got something to say that can't be put into a song. It's this. We absolutely *have* to find a way to beat the Zargons! They must have a weakness – and I've got a suspicion it has something to do with music.

Think about it guys. They have banned music and they're doing some kind of alien mind-wipe, so musicians and singers forget how to play and sing. Why? Well, I'm gonna make it my business to find out!

Finn the roadie

Like · Comment · Friend

Hey, I'm Finn and I have the best job in the world. I'm the *roadie* (that's road manager) for *GirlFriendZ*. Well, it *was* the best job until the Zargons arrived and we had to go on the run. Now my job is about getting the girls to their secret gigs *and* keeping them out of the Zargon's clutches! You see, the Zargon agents of MIB track down musicians and singers and take them off to the 'harmony' camps to have their minds wiped. Then, when they come out of the camps, they can't remember how to play or sing.

GirlFriendZ are the last band left, so MIB are desperate to catch them. If they do that, then that really *will* be the day music dies. But I'm never going to let that happen!

The Zargons

The Zargons are an alien race from the Andromeda galaxy. They have developed advanced technology that enables their starships to travel faster than the speed of light.

They are humanoid in appearance and, contrary to popular opinion, they do not possess tentacles (or tails!). However, in certain conditions, their eyes glow like cats' eyes.

They are on a mission to eradicate all forms of music from the universe. To this end, the Zargons build 'harmony' camps on the planets they invade. Anyone with musical talent is taken to the camps by Zargon agents of MIB (*Music Is Banned*), where they are subjected to a process known as 'mind wiping'. The mind-wipe has the effect of making the musician or singer forget how to play or sing. In street slang this process is known as 'soul stealing'.

The main feature of the 'harmony' camps are the giant incinerators where musical instruments are destroyed.

It is believed that the Zargons' hatred of music stems from the fact that music is the only thing that has the power to defeat them. (See article: *vampires*, *garlic*, *crosses*.)

Prologue

'Thank you Wembley. It's been emotional.'

Kelly punched the air with her fist and 70,000 fans screamed back at her. Yaz, Olivia, Eve and Charlotte, the other members of *GirlFriendZ*, jumped up and down on the stage like hyperactive kangaroos. Waves of love washed over them from their fans. If they hadn't known they were the world's biggest band before this gig – they knew it now!

'Hey, listen to those guys,' yelled Charlotte.

'Yay, it's awesome,' Eve yelled back at her.

Olivia grinned like a cat with a bowl of double cream. 'It just doesn't get any better than this.'

'Yes it does,' said Yaz. 'This show's being beamed worldwide by satellite. Billions of people are going mad for us.'

* * * * * * *

Suddenly a huge shadow covered the stadium. The howling crowd fell silent. A giant starship hovered over Wembley.

At first people thought it was part of the show. But then a red laser light shot out from the ship and vapourised the Wembley

arch. A metallic voice rang out into the stunned silence.

'People of Earth, go to your homes and stay there. This is an order. Failure to obey will be punishable by death. This planet is now a province of the Zargon Empire.'

One

Gonnabe

A battered old van pulled into the car park of a large supermarket. Nobody gave it a second glance. It looked like a million other transit vans. But this one held a secret. Inside was *GirlFriendZ* – the world's most famous band. They were on the run from MIB.

MIB was the dreaded Zargon organisation dedicated to hunting down musicians and wiping their minds, so they forgot how to play and sing. Naturally, *GirlFriendZ* were top of MIB's most-wanted list.

Finn, the girls' road manager and driver, switched off the engine and turned to them.

'OK guys, you stay here while I go inside and buy us some food and drink.'

'No way, Finn,' said Kelly. 'We need to stretch our legs. We've been stuck inside this boneshaker for hours.'

Finn shrugged. 'Sorry, Kelly, but it's too big a risk.' He pulled his baseball cap down low over his face. 'No MIB agent checking the Satspy cameras is going to notice me, but you girls are a totally different ball-game.'

The girls groaned, but they knew Finn was right. He jumped out of the van and headed off. The girls lapsed into a moody silence. Eve flicked through the channels on a small digital radio, but all she could hear was static.

'Leave it, Eve,' snapped Charlotte. 'Since the invasion, MIB has shut down all the music stations.'

'Yeah, that's right,' agreed Yaz. 'All you can hear now is Zargon propaganda 24/7.'

But Yaz was wrong. Suddenly music burst out of the small speakers. And it wasn't just any music, it was *Gonnabe – GirlFriendZ'* biggest hit!

Two

Pirate Radio

The girls were stunned.

'Quick! Turn it off, Eve,' hissed Liv. 'We don't want anyone to hear it.'

'Yes we do,' said Charlotte. 'It's us and it's brilliant.'

'No don't turn it off, just turn it down,' said Kelly. Then she frowned. 'But who's broadcasting our stuff? They're just asking to be mind-wiped!'

'That's right,' said Yaz. 'MIB will pick up the broadcast, track it down and silence it.'

'*And* whoever it is who's playing it,' added Eve ominously.

Then, as the track came to an end, an excited voice came out through the speakers.

'Hey, guys, this is Captain Black, the pirate DJ. That's right. I'm the man MIB can't silence. I rule the airways and they don't know how or where to find me! So I'm going to keep on playing the sounds the Zargons don't want you to hear. And I know you want to hear more songs by *GirlFriendZ*. So here's another killer track.'

The opening beats to *Rapping Feet* filled the van.

Then Captain Black continued. 'I don't know if Kelly and co are out there listening but, if you are, I'd love to have you come on board and do a live show. That would really stick it to MIB. So, let's do it *GirlFriendZ*!'

Three

Ancient History

When Finn came back to the van the girls were buzzing with excitement. They told him what had just happened.

'We're going to do a live show on a pirate radio station,' said Eve.

'Yay, Captain Black the DJ is *sooo* cool,' said Yaz.

'He's pumping out our tunes and MIB are tearing their alien hair out 'cos they can't find him.' Charlotte flicked her fingers triumphantly.

'But there's only one problem,' said Kelly.

Finn raised his eyebrows. 'Only *one* problem?' he said sarcastically.

Kelly nodded. 'Yeah. *We* don't know how to find him either.'

The girls all looked expectantly at Finn. He held up his hands. 'Hey, why are you all staring at me like that?'

''Cos you're our roadie,' said Charlotte. 'You always know how to get us to the places we want to go.'

Finn sat back and folded his arms. 'Look, if MIB's top agents can't track this DJ down then I don't know how you think I'm supposed to do it.'

The girls said nothing. They just carried on looking at him, like kids looking at Father Christmas.

He sighed. 'OK. It's a long shot, but I've got an idea of where he might be.'

The girls high-fived each other. 'So where do you think he's hiding out?' asked Kelly.

Finn chewed on his lip and looked thoughtful. 'Well, my grandad told me that, way back in the day when he was a kid, there used to be DJs who broadcast music from an old fort out in the North Sea. They called themselves pirate DJs. Maybe Captain Black is the grandson of one of them.'

Charlotte nodded enthusiastically. 'That's got to be it.'

'Yeah,' said Yaz. 'And that's why he hasn't been caught – 'cos no way would MIB know about ancient history like that.'

'So don't just sit there, Mr Roadie. Get driving,' said Eve.

'That's right,' added Kelly. 'We've got a live show to do!'

Four

The Last DJ

'I think I'm going to be seasick.'
Charlotte's face turned green. 'I hate boats.'

'This isn't a boat, it's a dinghy,' said Eve.

Charlotte glowered at her. 'Whatever.'

The girls were crammed inside a small
rubber dinghy that was bouncing along
through the choppy waters of the North

Sea. They were heading towards a sinister-looking building. It squatted on top of four thick steel legs that rose up out of the sea, giving it the appearance of a malevolent and brooding monster.

'Wow, it's a creepy-looking place,' said Liv in a shaky voice. 'Finn, are you sure this is where Captain Black is hanging out?'

Finn shrugged. He manoeuvred the dinghy up to a ladder that extended down from the fort. 'Well, there's a motor boat moored here,' he answered. 'So that means someone's about.'

'Let's hope it's our favourite pirate DJ,' said Kelly.

'Hey, there's only one way to find out,' said Yaz, as she grabbed the ladder and began to clamber up the rungs. 'Last one on board has to walk the plank!'

'Huh, it's all right for her,' grumbled Charlotte. 'She used to be an acrobat. I just know I'm going to fall in the sea if I try and climb that ladder.'

But she didn't. And, one by one, the girls all made their way up onto the old fort. They stood on the decking feeling nervous.

The only sound they could hear was the lapping of the waves far below them. Suddenly, a door was thrown open and a man stood there framed in the light.

'Welcome aboard shipmates,' he boomed. 'I'm Captain Black – the last DJ on Planet Earth!'

Five

Making a Splash

Captain Black stepped out onto the decking. The moon came out from behind a cloud and in its light his eyes glowed a weird yellow colour, like a cat's.

The girls shrank away from him. Their backs came up against the rusty railing that was the only thing preventing them from falling off the fort and plunging 50 metres into the sea below.

'You're not a DJ,' said Kelly accusingly. 'You're a Zargon MIB agent!'

The agent nodded. 'I am indeed,' he said smoothly. 'And you girls have walked – or should I say *sailed* – straight into my trap!'

'But Zargons can't bear music,' said Eve. 'So how come you could listen to ours when you played it on the radio?'

The alien laughed. It was a harsh, grating, very unmusical sound. 'I didn't,' he said. 'I wore ear defenders.' He glanced out to sea and smiled. The girls turned and saw a boat filled with MIB agents racing across the water towards the fort.

'Get back down here pronto,' yelled Finn from the dinghy. 'We've got company!'

At once the girls started to scramble back down the ladder.

'Why the big hurry, *GirlFriendZ*?' said the alien. 'You can't escape.'

The MIB boat was now nearly at the fort. Kelly, Charlotte, Eve and Liv were back in the dinghy, but Yaz had stayed up on the deck.

'So why don't you try and catch me, Mr Pirate DJ? Maybe you can make me walk the plank.'

The alien lunged towards her, but Yaz used all her acrobatic skills to leap up onto the flimsy rail and somersault over his head.

The alien lost his balance and stumbled into the railing. It gave way under his weight and he went crashing through it and tumbled down through the air.

He landed with a tremendous crash in the MIB boat, smashing a big hole in it. Immediately it began to fill with water and sink.

Yaz slid down the ladder and stepped into the dinghy. As soon as she was on board, Finn ripped open the throttle and the dinghy surged away from the fort, leaving the MIB agents and Captain Black splashing about frantically in the icy water.

Eve looked back at them. 'Hey, Captain Black wasn't much of a pirate DJ, but he certainly made those MIB agents abandon ship!'

'Oh, funny girl,' said Liv.

'Yeah,' agreed Kelly. 'We had the last laugh this time. But those guys won't quit until either we're mind-wiped or they leave Earth.'

Charlotte groaned and held her stomach. Her face was a horrible green colour. 'Hey, guys, nothing can be worse than being sea-sick, so please can we just get back on dry land and then I'll worry about mind-wiping!'

Finn nodded and headed the dinghy towards the distant shore.

* * * * * * *

Meanwhile, back on the fort, the MIB agents sat at a table, shivering and dripping sea water onto the floor.

'This time our plan failed,' said the agent known as Captain Black. 'But, I promise

you, *GirlFriendZ*, you will not be so lucky
next time.'